DISCARDE

Anna,
the One and Only

Anna,
the One and Only

by Barbara M. Joosse

illustrated by Gretchen Will Mayo

J. B. Lippincott   New York

Typography by Joyce Hopkins
2 3 4 5 6 7 8 9 10

_____

Library of Congress Cataloging-in-Publication Data
Joosse, Barbara M.
    Anna, the one and only / by Barbara M. Joosse : illustrated
by Gretchen Will Mayo. — 1st ed.
        p.   cm.
    Summary: Third grader Anna Skoggen struggles to ex-
press her true personality, and finally finds a way to be
herself and become friends with her older sister, Kimberly.
    ISBN 0-397-32322-0 : $.   ISBN 0-397-32323-9 (lib.
bdg.) : $.
    [1. Self-perception—Fiction.   2. Sisters—Fiction.]   I.
Mayo, Gretchen, ill.   I. Title.
PZ7.J7435An   1988   88-890
Fic—dc19   CIP
                                                          AC

For good teachers everywhere,
including our Pat Borlen.

Contents

1 Egg Harbor   3
2 This Is Home   18
3 The Woe Child   34
4 "Call Me Chocolate"   44
5 In Trouble Everywhere   58
6 Luxury Day   71
7 Blood Sisters   85
8 Tryouts   96
9 "Break A Leg"   105
10 This Time For Anna   121

1
Egg Harbor

The car hadn't felt so crowded an hour ago. But now Anna felt it was impossible to move without bumping into Kimberly.

"Anna!" said Kimberly. "Will you please stop poking me with your elbow?"

Anna tried to hold still, but then she started thinking about moving into the new house and choosing her own room. She started thinking about Lake Michigan and sailing on it and fishing in it. She wondered about the neighbors and the new school. Anna wondered, most of all, if anyone would like her.

Anna bounced the bottoms of her legs on the seat, pressing them hard against the springy blue fabric, and then kicked them up again. She liked the way her legs, which were normally thin, became fat when she flattened them on the seat.

Ka-bong, ka-bong. Anna swung her head against the back of the seat. She was sweaty in the hot car and the breeze felt good.

There was a little swirly spot on the back of Anna's head where her reddish hair knotted up and stuck out. Now that swirly spot itched. It was hard to reach so far back, and Anna had to swing her arm way over her head.

"Mother, make her stop!" Kimberly cried.

Mom turned around to face the backseat. She was seat belted in, so she couldn't turn to face both girls. She could face one way or the other and she chose to face Anna's way.

"Anna," she said, her gray eyes stormy, "you're making this trip more difficult than it needs to be. Please sit still and eat something from your snack sack."

4

Anna would have been more than happy to eat something from her snack sack, but she'd eaten everything the first half hour of the trip.

Kimberly had not. Kimberly's snack sack was still full of grapes, string cheese, peanuts, two Snickers bars, and a pack of wintergreen mints. It remained sealed—crisply folded over twice—on Kimberly's lap.

Anna looked at Kimberly's sack longingly. Kimberly had written her name in swirling, delicate strokes with a fine purple marker. She had drawn a colorful pattern around her name in shades of pink, purple, and blue. There was no mistaking Kimberly's sack for Anna's, so Anna knew it was hopeless to try to switch them. She thought of the peanuts huddled inside, lonely, wishing for an eager mouth to gobble them up. Anna was sure they'd be happier in her tummy than Kimberly's. Kimberly didn't even like nuts especially.

"Do you want your nuts, Kimberly?" Anna asked.

"Yes," said Kimberly, flipping her smooth, long hair over her shoulder. Kimberly combed her hair several times a day, so she never had a swirly knot at the back.

"Do you want *all* of them?"

"Yes," said Kimberly, smoothing a wrinkle out of her sundress.

"I'll trade you everything that's in my sack for six of your peanuts," said Anna.

"Okay," said Kimberly. She opened her bag and carefully counted out six nuts and gave them to Anna. Feeling a little guilty, Anna handed her empty snack sack to Kimberly. She didn't think Kimberly would fall for her trick, and she didn't really like tricking her. Still, she wanted the nuts, and there was no turning back.

Kimberly laid Anna's sack on the seat.

Why didn't Kimberly open the sack? Is she going to show it to Mom, to prove what a sneak I am? Maybe she's going to save it for last, as a special treat. It would be terrible to look forward to more snack and then find none. It would be worse than saving a triple-nut peanut for last and finding it spoiled.

Anna couldn't stand it! "Kimberly," she confessed, "there's nothing in the bag. It's empty."

"I know," said Kimberly.

"You know?" cried Anna. "Then why did you trade six nuts for an empty bag?"

"Because," said Kimberly, looking at Anna with clear, blue eyes, "if I'd eaten all my snacks, I would have liked someone to give me an extra treat."

Kimberly really *was* nice. Everyone said so. That's one reason why her teachers liked her and why she was always winning things like the Good Citizenship Award. That was also one of the main reasons Anna didn't like her.

It was bad enough to have a big sister who was beautiful and artistic. It was bad enough to hear "Kimberly this" and "Kimberly that" all the time. But it was too much when Kimberly was nice and understanding and—worst of all—patient with her.

And that's why, even though Anna was still chewing Kimberly's nuts, she reached out and accidentally punched Kimberly on the arm.

"Ouch!" cried Kimberly, grabbing her arm. "That hurt!"

"I'm sorry," said Anna.

"No you aren't," said Kimberly. "You aren't

7

sorry at all. You meant to hit me."

Daddy swerved the car to the shoulder of the road. Anna listened to the gravel ping up against the metal. She heard the pings slow down and finally stop. She heard all that very well because nobody was saying a word. Daddy unbuckled his seat belt and faced his daughters.

"Kimberly," he said, looking at his older daughter. "Anna," he said, turning to his younger. "We are all nervous about moving. We will be living in a new state. We will be living in a new town. We will be living in a new house. . . ."

Daddy always used short sentences when he was angry. He felt, Anna thought, that if you were dumb enough to do something wrong you were too dumb to understand long sentences.

". . . Some of us will attend new schools. Some of us will work at new jobs. It would be nice if we would do all of this without animosity."

When Daddy used a big word like "animosity," Anna knew he was about to give a long speech, almost like the editorials he wrote for the newspaper. Daddy was a newspaper editor. They were moving to Egg Harbor, in fact, so he could become editor of the *Door County Advocate.*

"Sisters should grow closer during times of stress. You should strive to understand each other and be patient and understanding. I can't believe you . . ."

Anna looked at Daddy. It seemed she was always disappointing Mom and Daddy, and they were always trying to improve her character.

She didn't want to think about that, so she thought about something else while Daddy's voice floated somewhere above her. She thought about the wonderful tree they had in their old backyard. You could climb up and up and hide in the branches. Anna felt she could fly when she was in that tree. She wished she were flying now, looking down from the sky at the little blue car full of Skoggens.

The talking stopped. Daddy turned away

from them and belted himself back in. "We can all learn a valuable lesson from this," he said, pulling back onto the road.

Well, that's over, thought Anna. Anna hated it when Daddy was unhappy with her. She wanted Mom and Daddy to be proud of her, just as they were proud of Kimberly. No, she wanted them to be most proud of her and just a little proud of Kimberly. But the only time they seemed to be proud of her was last year when she sold the most Girl Scout cookies in her troop. The rest of the time they seemed to be worried about her or angry with her.

Anna poked the cuticle on her thumbnail back so the moon showed. It was nice to have a moon on your own thumb whenever you wanted it.

Anna looked at the back of Daddy's head and thought. Daddy's light-brown hair was thick and stiff. He parted it neatly on one side. No matter what happened—no matter how far he jogged or how hard the wind blew—his hair always looked the same. It was so stiff it looked like he combed it with school paste.

His lap was bony, while Mom's was soft.

Mom was always trying to fatten him up, but she only succeeded in adding a few pounds to her own weight.

Even though Daddy's lap was bony, it was still a wonderful place to sit. Anna loved the smell of his work shirt—a little bit of Daddy and a little bit of printer's ink. She loved to sit with her nose next to his chest while Daddy wrapped his long arms around her. Anna had a stuffed monkey that had very long arms with Velcro hands. When you wrapped that monkey around something, it held on tight. You could never shake it loose. Anna felt that way about Daddy.

They drove a long, long time before Mom finally said, "We're almost in Door County. Let's watch for the sign."

"Is there a prize for the one who sees the sign first?" asked Anna.

"Sure," said Mom. Digging around in her purse, she pulled out a lipstick.

Lipstick! The prize will be lipstick, Anna thought.

But when Mom pulled out a little mirror and began putting the lipstick on her own lips,

11

Anna began to doubt whether the prize would be lipstick.

"What?" asked Anna, stretching over Mom's seat to look into her purse.

"What what?" asked Mom, confused.

"What's the prize?" asked Anna.

Mom snapped the lipstick cover back on the tube and dropped it into her purse. She rummaged around until she found a half-eaten tube of mints.

"The prize will be mints," said Mom.

Anna thought the mints weren't a very good prize, but she still wanted to win. She knelt on the seat and searched through the front window for the sign. When she saw a sign that said WELCOME TO DOOR COUNTY, she shouted, "The sign! There it is! I win!"

Mom handed her the mints just as Daddy pulled the car to the side of the road and picked up his camera.

"Everybody out! We're going to take a picture," he said. Anna was out of the car first, hopping in the thin grass next to the road.

"I won I won I won," she sang.

Mom and Kimberly remained in the car a

little longer. Mom fluffed her short, curly hair with her fingers. Kimberly combed hers.

While everybody gathered in front of the sign, Daddy set the camera on the car hood. Mom stood in the middle, with Kimberly to one side and Anna to the other. She looked at Anna, who had milk from breakfast and chocolate from the snack sack on her face, and pulled a tissue out of her pocket.

"Stick out your tongue," she said to Anna. Mom scraped her tissue along Anna's tongue and then scrubbed Anna's face clean. Then she combed Anna's hair with her fingers, quickly smoothing Anna's straight, red hair away from her face.

"We're ready," she said.

Daddy set the delay button on the camera and ran back just in time to put his arms over the backs of their shoulders.

Click.

Anna ran back to the car while everyone else walked. Daddy was the last one to close his door because it took him the longest to fold himself into his seat. He turned the key and the car rumbled to a start.

"The tank's getting empty," Daddy said.

Like my stomach, thought Anna, who was desperate enough to start eating her prize.

They had driven only a short while when Mom said, "Here's a nice station."

Anna thought one station was as nice as another. They all had gas, didn't they?

"It looks like it has nice, clean rest rooms," Mom said. Mom liked nice, clean rest rooms. Anna preferred nice, cold soda machines.

Everybody got out of the car. "Can I have some money for soda?" Anna asked.

Daddy pulled out some change from his pocket. "Don't you think you'd better go to the rest room first?" he asked.

"No," said Anna, "I don't need to go."

She ran to the soda machine, squeaking her tennis shoes on the hot pavement.

Chink-chink! The machine hummed cheerfully while Anna made up her mind between root beer and orange. *Chunk!* A can of root beer slid out, cool and frosty.

"Anna, have you used the rest room?" asked Mom. "It's nice and clean."

"No," said Anna, peeling the tab off the can. "I don't have to go."

The truth was, Anna had to go, a little. She walked to the car, careful not to spill her soda.

"We'll be in Egg Harbor in an hour," said Daddy, starting the car.

An hour, thought Anna, is a million years away.

Anna took several gulps of her soda and burped quietly. She knew she'd be a lot more comfortable if she could stretch her legs, but to do that, she'd have to sit right next to Kimberly. Anna plopped next to Kimberly and stretched her legs, cramming Kimberly tightly into the corner. Kimberly rose slightly off the seat and bumped sharply into Anna.

"Ouch!" Anna stared at her sister. "You didn't have to do *that*," she whispered, so Daddy wouldn't hear. "I was just changing positions."

"Yes I *did* have to do that," whispered Kimberly, "and no, you weren't just changing positions."

The sisters glowered at each other.

Finally, Kimberly said, reasonably, "Here's what we're going to do. I'll run my belt right down the middle of the backseat. Then each of us must stay in her area."

Kimberly took off her belt and stretched it out.

Anna hated it when Kimberly was reasonable and patient. However, this did sound like a good idea. She thought about it and said, "I live in Anna Land, country of wild beasts and deep, dark caves."

"And I live in the Land of Kimberly, home of tropical beauty. Waterfalls, wild heather, peacocks. There is no ruler here; we're all fair and cooperative."

"Anna Land has thieves and pirates."

"The Land of Kimberly has concerts every afternoon."

"Anna Land is mostly purple."

"The Land of Kimberly is mauve."

"In Anna Land," said Anna, "there are many wild animals, but they're all my friends. I am the ruler and everyone obeys me. I rule, of course, with kindness. I am beloved by all."

"How appropriate," Kimberly said. "Queen of the Beasts."

2

This Is Home

The new house was old and light gray in color. There were lots of cherry trees and there was a big, thick tree, taller than Anna's old tree, right by the house. There was a porch with a porch swing, a slanted cellar door and—most wonderful of all—a little walk-around porch on the roof that Mom said was called a widow's walk.

Anna hopped from foot to foot while Mom looked for the house keys. "They're in here somewhere," she promised, brightly.

"I have to go to the bathroom," Anna said, knowing that would make Mom hurry. After pulling out lipstick, a notebook, a mirror, and a small packet of tissue, Mom jingled the keys triumphantly. "Voilà!" she exclaimed.

But when she tried to insert the key in the lock, she discovered it was the wrong one. She tried another key. "I'm sure this is it," she promised as she jammed the third key into the lock upside down. With the key right side up, Mom tried again. This time Anna heard the key slide in and turn with a satisfying click. Finally, the red door swung open and Anna plunged inside.

The dining room! It had lots of cupboards and a slickly polished floor. Anna skidded across, riding a small rag rug. She imagined all the wonderful birthday parties she'd have in this room, and she thought about how the ceiling would look with crepe-paper streamers.

As Anna skidded through the dining room, she noticed the bathroom but decided she could wait until she had toured the house.

The kitchen had yellow, gauzy curtains that would make it look like the sun was shining even when it wasn't. There was a pantry with a door you could close for privacy if you were eating a cookie when you shouldn't. There was a skinny little cupboard with its own ironing board hidden inside. And there was a tiny door that covered a narrow tunnel that led to the outside: a milk chute. It was just big enough for Anna to fit through. Her own private exit!

Anna crawled into the tight little tunnel, determined to reach the little door on the other end. At last she felt the door with her fingers, inched a fraction further and punched it open with her fist. Anna tried to slide through to the outside. She got as far as her head, but her shoulders and the rest of her wouldn't come along. The tunnel must be narrower on the outside, she decided. She would have to crawl back.

Anna heaved and pushed, but the harder she tried the less she moved. And the less she moved the more she sweated. Anna was jammed tight—her head sticking out of one end, and her legs out of the other. It was hot and stuffy in the tunnel, and not the least of Anna's problems was that she *really* had to go to the bathroom now. How she wished she had gone to the bathroom first!

"Mom! Dad!" yelled Anna. "Somebody help!"

She waited, but no one came to rescue her. She yelled again, louder.

"HELP! HELP! HE-ELP!"

At last she heard the muffled sound of Daddy's voice. "Anna? Anna, where are you?"

Anna heard steps coming closer, closer still. Then she heard laughter. Anna thought they were very rude. She wouldn't have laughed if she'd found someone stuck inside a milk chute, especially when the someone had to go to the bathroom.

It would serve them right if she wet her pants and the milk chute smelled terrible for the rest of the time they lived in this house!

"Don't worry, Anna, we'll have you out in no time," Daddy said. Mom was outside, pushing Anna's shoulders gently toward the kitchen. Daddy pulled at her legs until at long last she slid free.

21

"It was awful in there," she told Daddy as he eased her down to the kitchen floor.

"Well, you're out now," said Daddy. "Just don't try crawling through there again."

"I won't," promised Anna, thinking that she really wouldn't unless it was absolutely necessary, and then only on a cooler day. Anna was sure she wouldn't have gotten stuck if she hadn't been so sweaty. Kimberly, Anna knew, would *never* have gotten stuck in the milk chute.

Anna walked to the bathroom with painful slowness to show she wasn't in any particular hurry. It was bad enough to have to be rescued from the milk chute and to be laughed at. Anna didn't want to look even more babyish by running to the bathroom.

When Anna came out, she headed upstairs, taking the steps two at a time. There was a long hall with several rooms. Anna looked in the first, a large room with brown carpet. There was a big window with curtains that hung to the floor. It would be fun, Anna thought, to stand behind the curtains and pretend it was a stage. Next was a medium-sized bedroom with a large closet. The third room was a bathroom with a clothes chute and a cushy toilet seat.

The last bedroom, a very small one, had a low ceiling and flowered wallpaper. The ceiling was so low it made Anna feel bigger. And you had to push the windows out to open them, like in a fairy tale! Anna cranked the knob down and swung the window open, feeling the fresh lake breeze fill the little room—her little room!—with puffs of summer air.

Anna opened the door next to the closet. Inside was a short, dark stairway. Anna felt along the rough side, slowly climbing five steps to the top. Her heart was beating wildly because she just knew what had to be at the top. Still, she wanted to take her time, to make the feeling at the end all the better. Anna reached for the doorknob, turned it, and flung the door open.

Anna rushed outside, spinning and twirling with excitement. There was a wide porch, wide enough to play on, wide enough to *dance* on. Over it all were the green, lacy branches of the big oak tree. A spiky metal fence circled the edge of the widow's walk. Anna walked to it now. How wonderfully high! Anna could see most of Egg Harbor and some of Lake Michigan. People hurried along the sidewalk, stopping in the shops, climbing into the boats along the edge of the lake. There was a boy riding a bike. There was a neighbor hanging out wash. Anna watched them all, happy to be part of such a busy town.

Anna looked toward the sun-brightened cliffs on the edge of town. She looked out over Lake Michigan and watched the colors move and change on the water. And everywhere there were sea gulls, spinning and diving and floating. Anna leaned over the rusty, old fence.

"Hi, Mom!" she yelled. "Look at me!"

"Anna!" cried Mom. "Be careful up there . . . PLEASE! And don't lean over the fence. It's old and dangerous!"

Anna stopped leaning because Mom told her to and because Mom was still watching. But Anna knew the fence was safe. She shook it to prove her point and the fence did not break loose. Mom was just a scaredy-cat. Anna decided not to lean on the fence anymore when Mom was watching. And when Mom wasn't

24

watching she would only lean on it when it was absolutely necessary.

"Anna," said Mom, more calmly now, "please come down and help us unload the car."

"Okay," said Anna cheerfully. She looked at the thick, old tree. It would be a cinch to climb and the quickest way down.

"Don't climb down that tree!" Mom called from the driveway.

How did Mom know what Anna was thinking?

Anna made her voice sound hurt, as though she wouldn't have considered climbing down that tree, not in a million years. "I wasn't going to," she said.

And she wouldn't. Not unless it was absolutely necessary, like if a small kitten was stuck and needed rescuing or if Anna was late for school and the bus were honking.

It was fun to unpack the boxes, and to decide where everything would go. The big things would come in the moving van the next day, but the Skoggens had taken some supplies and a few special things with them. A box full of picture albums. Plants, coffee maker, peanut butter, paper plates and cups, and toilet paper. The cooler. Sleeping bags. Daddy's fishing pole. Mom's jewelry. Anna's bug net.

Kimberly had packed several special things. Her viola, foreign doll collection, trophies, paints, records and autographed poster of the Milwaukee Ballet Company. It seemed to Anna that Kimberly had many more special things than anyone else.

"Look at all this stuff! Almost everything is yours," said Anna.

"Mom said I could bring these things," said Kimberly.

"We were only supposed to bring *special* things," Anna said.

"All these things are special to me," said Kimberly.

"Special," said Anna, "means a few."

"I'm sorry," said Kimberly. "If I'd known you wanted to take more things I wouldn't have taken so much."

"Well next time I get to take the most," said

Anna. Anna knew that there probably wouldn't be a next time. The Skoggens planned to stay in Egg Harbor a long, long time.

After everything was carried inside and Mom and Kimberly began dusting the empty bookshelves, Anna went back up to the widow's walk. She sat down, leaning her back against the house wall. It was almost dusk. Anna looked over the spiky fence at the hills and water below.

Egg Harbor had looked so busy before—full of people and sunshine. Now it was still and shadowy.

This is a new house and a new town, Anna thought, but I'm still the same old me. Anna pulled her knees up to her chin. Her skin smelled warm and familiar. Anna looked at her bumpy knee with the fuzzy hairs on it. Why does Kimberly get to shave her legs, and I don't?

Why did Kimberly get to bring the most special things? Why does Kimberly have the most treasures? Why is Kimberly so reasonable? And why do I always do dumb things, like getting stuck in that milk chute? And why,

why do Mom and Dad have to be proud of Kimberly and not me?

Anna stayed on the widow's walk until the sun touched the lake. Then she walked through her bedroom and down the stairs. The darkening house felt chilly and strange, full of unfamiliar things.

In the living room, Mom, Dad and Kimberly were chattering away, busy arranging a picnic supper. Anna watched from the shadowy stairway.

"I'm going to start my job at the bookmobile the day the girls start school." Mom slid the rubber band off the bag of potato chips.

"What are you going to wear?" asked Kimberly.

"My red, I think. Librarians should always wear cheery colors."

"A characteristic like cheerfulness comes from inside," said Daddy. "You shouldn't be so influenced by clothing."

Mom pulled back the edge of the rubber band and snapped Daddy's leg. She never let him get away with newspaper talk.

Mom noticed Anna. "Are you hungry, dear?" asked Mom.

"Yes," Anna said.

Mom and Anna had prepared the food the day before and had packed it carefully in a cooler. Now Kimberly spread a towel on the living room floor while Daddy heaped a pile of cold fried chicken on a paper plate. Anna spooned cucumber salad, her favorite, into a bowl.

"How about a fire?" asked Daddy.

"Supper by firelight," said Mom cheerfully. "How perfect for our first night in Egg Harbor."

Daddy carried an armload of wood into the house. He made a little mound of kindling, and heaped some larger logs on top. "Girls," he said, "do you know that our new county is a peninsula?"

"Yes," said Kimberly.

"A peninsula, of course, is a body of land surrounded on three parts by water—the water, of course, being Lake Michigan."

Daddy struck a wooden match and touched it to the kindling. "You'll notice that the state of Wisconsin is shaped like a mittened hand, and Door County is the thumb." Daddy blew at the tiny fire until the flames lapped the edges of the white birch logs.

Anna knew Daddy was wrong. They had crossed a bridge to get here, and if Door County was connected to the rest of Wisconsin by land, why did they have to cross a bridge? If she mentioned the bridge, though, she was sure Daddy would give her a geography lesson. So, instead she sang:

> *Thumb in the thumbhole,*
> *fingers all together.*
> *This is the song*
> *we sing in mitten weather!*

The mitten song was one Anna had learned in kindergarten, and she still liked it.

After dinner, Anna and Kimberly roasted marshmallows.

"We'll sleep in sleeping bags tonight," Mom said, yawning.

"In front of the fireplace," cried Anna.

31

"All in a row," said Kimberly.

"All together," said Dad.

Mom kicked off her shoes and stretched her feet toward the fire.

"But tomorrow when we get our beds I'm moving into the little room with the flowered wallpaper," said Anna.

"What?" said Kimberly, nearly dropping her marshmallow into the fire. "That's *my* room! Mother, you said I could have it."

Anna looked at her mother. "It's true," Mom said, "I told Kimberly she could have it."

"Nobody asked me," said Anna, her eyes getting hot. "Nobody asked me which room I wanted. Nobody ever asks me anything! I wanted that room!"

Daddy cleared his throat. "We will have to find an equitable solution." He reached toward Anna. "I think you girls should share the room."

"But it's too small," said Kimberly.

"It *is* small," said Mom, "but I think we can fit everything in. And then we can use the third bedroom for a guest room."

32

Anna stopped crying and sniffed loudly to clear her runny nose.

"Anna's so sloppy," said Kimberly. "She'll never keep the room neat!"

"Maybe she'll learn to follow your example," said Mom.

"But Anna snores, and tosses and turns. She'll keep me awake," said Kimberly.

Anna stood up and said, "Kimberly talks in her sleep."

"I do not," said Kimberly.

"Do too," said Anna.

"Girls!" said Daddy. "There will be no fighting tonight. It's settled. Mom and I will sleep in the big room and Kimberly and Anna will sleep in the small one. The middle room will be for guests."

Anna sat on her sleeping bag and slid inside. The snug little room would be hers after all, even if she did have to share it with Kimberly.

Anna was beginning to feel very sleepy.

She didn't even notice when Daddy pulled her sleeping bag gently up around her shoulders or when Mom tenderly kissed her cheek.

3

The Woe Child

The moving van had arrived, bringing all the things that made the Skoggens' new house home. Pictures were hung, books were set out, and closets were filled. Mom and Kimberly had arranged the furniture in the living room five times, until they found the right place for everything.

The Skoggen house began to look lived-in. The refrigerator was covered with notes and a wildflower sketch that Kimberly had done in colored pencils.

The girls were lying on their beds, dressed in pajamas, ready for the first day of school the next day.

Anna held up a jam jar full of flies. "Would you like to see my dead fly collection?" she asked.

"Later," said Kimberly, without looking up. Kimberly was sketching the lighthouse the family had visited the day before.

Anna shook the jar to make it look as though the flies were alive and buzzing inside.

"Look," she cried, "the flies have come back to life, like zombies."

Kimberly was erasing the waves, brushing the eraser crumbs quickly off the paper. Her hands moved fast.

Anna shook the jar of flies in front of Kimberly's face. "I vant to suck your blood," she said.

"What?" said Kimberly, finally looking up. "Oh, gross, Anna," she said.

Anna shoved the jar under the covers. "How many flies do you think I have now?" she asked.

"I don't know," said Kimberly, and went back to fixing the waves. Anna thought the waves looked more like a bumpy blanket, but she didn't say so.

"Guess," said Anna. "Guess how many flies!"

Kimberly put down her sketch. "Twenty. You had fifteen when we left Rockford, so now I think you have twenty."

"Forty-seven!" cried Anna, triumphantly pulling out the jar.

The new house had a lot of flies, and they were getting slow and drowsy because it was almost September. Anna used her hand to catch the flies because it was more challenging. You really had to sneak up on the flies. You had to move slowly and come down from the back.

Anna shook some of the flies into a plastic bag. Then she tucked the bag of flies into her pencil box where she could look at them if she felt lonely at school. She put the jar with the flies on the bookshelf. The shelf was full of Kimberly's trophies and art projects, sheet music, and art supplies. Besides books, the fly jar was the only thing on the shelf that was Anna's. Anna wanted to make sure people knew the jar was *hers*. She didn't want anyone to think this was just Kimberly's shelf. She poked around in a box of felt markers until she found one that wasn't dried out. The lime-green one was okay. She printed out ANNA'S DEAD FLY COLLECTION as carefully as she could, and set the jar in the middle of the shelf, next to Kimberly's foreign doll collection.

"Lights out," called Mom from downstairs. "School tomorrow."

Anna didn't need to be reminded about school. She'd been worrying about the first day of school all week, and tomorrow was it.

Kimberly crumpled her lighthouse drawing into a tight, little wad and threw it at the wastebasket. When it missed, she didn't pick it up. Then she turned out the light.

Soon Anna's eyes were used to the darkness, and she could see the moon and the stars through the moon window. The moon window was just a regular window, but you could see the moon through it. The moon always seemed friendly—like it was in the sky just for Anna. Anna always liked watching it before she fell asleep.

"Anna, are you nervous about school tomorrow?" asked Kimberly softly.

Anna thought about saying no, but the moon and the stars made her feel closer to Kimberly. "Yes, a little," she said.

"Me too," said Kimberly. Anna knew Kimberly couldn't be nervous. But it was nice of her to say it to make Anna feel better.

"I'm going to take some of my flies to school," said Anna.

"That's nice," said Kimberly, yawning. "You never know when you'll need a couple of dead flies."

Anna waited to fall asleep. She always tossed and flipped to find a comfortable spot before she went to sleep. But tonight she couldn't find one. Kimberly was already sleeping; little snoring sounds were coming from her bed.

Ha! thought Anna. Kimberly does snore! She couldn't wait to announce it at breakfast the next morning.

Anna flipped onto her back. She scratched her head, and she crossed her legs. She took a long, deep breath and let it out slowly.

Mom was playing "Malagueña" on the piano downstairs. It was a fast, thumping melody and made Anna think of horses. When the melody was over the house became very still. Anna couldn't even hear Mom and Daddy talking downstairs. She wondered if they had gone for a walk and left them alone. All alone in a new house just before the first day of school!

Anna thought about all the third graders walking to school tomorrow. She thought of them walking in twos and threes, happily talking about the summer. Most of them would have best friends, and all of them would have some friends. Some would even wear the same clothes, the way best friends sometimes do.

Anna looked out of the moon window. Now the moon didn't look cozy. It looked cold and mean, like an eye that didn't blink. Anna grabbed her monkey and wrapped his Velcro arms around her. They had been in Egg Harbor for over a week and Anna had not made a single friend. But then, who would be friends with such a plain person?

That's the thing, thought Anna. I'm plain, much too plain. I wish I were beautiful, like Kimberly. And talented. I wish I had trophies to prove what a talented person I am.

Why, even Mom and Dad liked Kimberly

better! How she wanted them to look at her the way they looked at Kimberly!

Anna thought of this rhyme from her nursery rhyme book:

Monday's child is fair of face,
Tuesday's child is full of grace,
Wednesday's child is full of woe,
Thursday's child has far to go,
Friday's child is loving and giving,
Saturday's child works hard for a living,
But the child that's born on the Sabbath day,
Is bonny and blithe, and good and gay.

Just my luck, thought Anna. Kimberly was born on Sunday, the Sabbath day. And I was born on Wednesday, the woe day. I wish *I* was the Sabbath child, not Kimberly.

Kimberly is beautiful. I am plain. Kimberly's gifted in the arts, and I'm gifted in nothing. Kimberly's good, and I get into trouble. Mom and Dad are proud of Kimberly, and they worry about me. Anna's stomach felt cold and icy, like water that's just about to freeze over. How could she ever make friends as just plain Anna?

Anna lay in bed a long, long time. Slowly

41

the worst feelings began to blow away, like smoke. Still, Anna couldn't sleep. She pulled the blanket over her head, breathing the stuffy air under the covers. Anna thought she'd have to lie awake all night. Then she would go to school with dark eyes and messy hair, and everyone in third grade would know she hadn't been to sleep. Then what would she say? Anna flipped the covers off her head.

She could say she was an orphan who lived alone and had to clean houses at night for a living.

She could say she was a junior member of the rescue squad, and they had many victims to save at night.

She could say she was an artist, and did her best work at night. That sounded better than the truth! It made Anna sound interesting. It cheered her up just to think about it.

The thing about a new town, thought Anna suddenly, is that nobody knows you. Anna zipped the rough part of her toenail along the sheet. *Zip zip.* Nobody knows I'm plain. Nobody knows I don't have trophies or that I'm messy and get into trouble. *Zip zip.* In a new town, I can be anybody I want. *Zip zip zip.* I won't be a woe child anymore. I'll be a Sabbath child! I'll be bonny and blithe and good and gay! I'll be jangly and bright and fancy! I'll be so fancy that everyone will want to be my friend.

Anna sighed, satisfied. She ran to her dresser and pulled out the nail clippers. She clipped off the jagged part of her toenail, then closed the shade on the moon window and settled back into bed. When she fell asleep, she dreamed of Anna, the Sabbath child.

4

"Call Me Chocolate"

Ffip-ffip-ffip-ffip!

"Anna!" yelled Kimberly. "Can't you open the shades without making a racket?"

"Okay," said Anna, thinking the racket was a cheerful way to start the day as a Sabbath child.

Anna put on her corduroy jumper. She didn't intend to wear it to school—it was much too plain—but Anna didn't want Kimberly to see her dressed as a Sabbath child. She would think Anna was silly. She looked over at Kimberly.

Kimberly was still in bed, covers up to her neck. Her eyes were dark and her cheeks were pale.

If Kimberly's sick, thought Anna, I can take care of her. I can show her how sweet and faithful I am, now that I'm a Sabbath child. "Are you sick, Kimberly?" asked Anna, in the kind of voice she supposed a nurse would use.

"No," said Kimberly.

"Then why are you still in bed? Is something wrong?" Anna felt Kimberly's forehead for fever.

"Leave me alone!" said Kimberly. "I'm tired, that's all."

Anna knew Kimberly wasn't tired. Anna had been awake most of the night and knew that Kimberly had been sleeping, even snoring. Maybe Kimberly doesn't want me to watch while she gets dressed, thought Anna. Kimberly is getting breasts now, and maybe she doesn't want me to look at them. A Sabbath child would be considerate. Anna decided to leave Kimberly alone.

Downstairs, Anna set the table, eager to show everyone how helpful she was. Everyone loves a Sabbath child, and Anna was sure that now everyone would love her. She set down the plates and made sure she put the knives and spoons to the right. She folded the napkins and arranged them in the orange juice glasses.

"My!" said Mom, coming into the kitchen. "Look at this!" Mom walked around the table, admiring Anna's work. Anna grinned. It felt good to be the one who had done a nice thing.

Anna toasted the bread while Mom made eggs, and she got to yell, "Breakfast!" because she helped make it.

Daddy walked down the stairs quickly, his hair combed crisply, smelling of shampoo and deodorant.

Kimberly came down last, slowly walking down the stairs. She sat at her place, across from Anna.

"Well," exclaimed Daddy, "don't my girls look lovely today?"

Anna wanted to tell Mom and Daddy about Kimberly snoring. She wanted to show them how Kimberly's mouth had hung open and snores came out. But she knew a Sabbath child wouldn't do it. But, if she didn't say anything, how would they know she was being nice? So Anna leaned across the table and whispered to Kimberly, "I heard you snoring last night, but I'm not going to tell."

"I don't snore," whispered Kimberly.

"Yes," insisted Anna, "you do. You snore like this." Anna threw her head back, dropped her jaw open, and snored loudly.

"What was that?" asked Daddy. "A wild animal or a banshee?"

"It was me," said Anna, looking at Kimberly to see if she was grateful that Anna had not mentioned her snoring. Kimberly didn't look very grateful.

Mom, Daddy, and Anna talked about the day. Kimberly was quiet, mostly, and Anna wondered if you became more quiet when you grew breasts.

"Wash your face, Anna," said Mom, as Anna ran upstairs to change. "And comb your hair! Don't forget the back!" Mom shouted.

"And hurry," yelled Daddy. "I want to take your picture."

Anna forgot about that! Daddy always took

47

their picture on the first day of school. How was she going to hide her Sabbath child outfit?

Anna thought about it as she took off her clothes and jammed them in a drawer. Then she put on Sabbath child clothes: a swirly skirt and Kimberly's beautiful white lace blouse. Anna knew Kimberly would normally not let her wear the blouse. But she was sure Kimberly would let her if she knew she was a Sabbath child.

Next Anna put on several jangly bracelets, three necklaces, and two rings. She also put on lip balm that was a little pinkish. She put it on thick enough so it almost looked like lipstick. Anna was very, very careful not to get any on Kimberly's blouse.

Anna had figured out a way to hide her Sabbath child clothes for the picture. She would wear her rain slicker over everything, and she would press her lips together so no one would see the lip balm.

Kimberly and Anna stood next to the big tree for the picture.

"Take your coat off, Anna, so we can see

your school dress," said Daddy, adjusting the camera.

"Is it supposed to rain today?" asked Mom, looking at the bright, sunny sky, and then at Anna's rain slicker.

"I think I heard it on the radio," said Anna, between her pressed-together lips.

"Here comes the bus!" said Mom.

Daddy quickly snapped the picture, and Kimberly and Anna ran to the end of their driveway.

The bus was pretty full, but there were a couple of empty seats near the back, so Kimberly and Anna sat in them. Anna didn't really want to watch all the children having fun and not be part of it so she looked down at her lap. She ran her finger back and forth across her slippery slicker. Soon she saw Kimberly's hand reach over to hold hers. Anna held Kimberly's hand gratefully..

When the bus got to Gibraltar School, Anna said good-bye to Kimberly and waited outside until almost everyone was in. Then she walked inside the shiny orange doors. Anna hung up her slicker on a hook outside her classroom. She looked at her lacy blouse and fancy jewelry and turned a little so her skirt would twirl. She was ready for life as a Sabbath child.

Anna walked into the room as the bell rang. She was shining with jewelry.

"Look at her!" said one boy.

"Holy cow!" said another boy.

Anna waited on the edge of the classroom, not sure where she should sit. Of course, a Sabbath child would walk right in and choose a seat, but Anna didn't want to sit at someone else's desk. So she waited until Miss Crystal noticed her.

Anna was glad Mom had taken her to meet her teacher last week. Miss Crystal had reddish hair, like Anna's, except that it was curly. Now she walked over to Anna, her high heels tapping crisply on the floor, and held out her hand. "Hello again, Anna. I'm so glad you'll be with us! You look like you're going to make this class very interesting!"

Now *that's* the kind of thing Anna liked to hear!

Miss Crystal led Anna to the front of the

class. "Class!" she said. "I want you to meet a new student who has come to us from Rockford, Illinois."

Everyone looked at Anna, except for one girl who was rolling her pencil down her desktop. Anna pointed one toe, and put her hand on her hip, the way she'd seen movie stars do in pictures.

Miss Crystal put an arm around Anna's shoulder, as though they were already friends. "Everyone please welcome our new friend, Anna Skoggen."

Miss Crystal pointed out Anna's desk, and Anna walked to her seat, letting her heels tap on the floor like Miss Crystal's.

Miss Crystal began roll call. "Stephanie Bolter."

"Here."

"Allen Durran."

"Here."

"Kirsten Olafson."

"Here."

"Anna Skoggen."

Anna said, "Please call me Chocolate," in a loud, clear voice.

51

"Did you say . . . Chocolate?" asked Miss Crystal, her eyebrows squeezing together.

"Yes," said Anna, a little less clearly.

"Isn't your name Anna Skoggen?"

"Well, my name is Anna, but everyone calls me Chocolate." It was good to have a nickname, thought Anna, and Chocolate sounded like a good one. Everyone liked chocolate!

"However did you get such an unusual name?" asked Miss Crystal, sitting on the edge of her desk.

Anna thought fast. "It's a long, long, *long* story," she said finally, because she couldn't think of anything to say. She started to unpack her backpack and arranged her things in her desk. First she put the tissue box in the corner of her desk, and the notebooks in the front. Then she reached for the rest. The last armload was heavy and wobbly. Anna lifted it very carefully, but the three-ring binder got tangled in one of her bracelets!

Blam! Anna's lunch money, three-ring binder, and pencil box crashed to the floor, scattering all over the aisle.

What a mess!

Anna quickly picked up her lunch money and snapped her binder shut. But by the time she noticed her open pencil box, everyone was staring at the plastic bag full of flies.

"Hey! What's in that plastic bag?" asked a boy.

Anna tried to scoop up the bag quickly.

"Flies," said another boy.

"Dead flies," said a girl.

"Are you going to eat them?" asked another girl, making a face.

Anna jammed the flies into the far corner of her desk. She didn't want to talk about them and she didn't want to look at them. After that, it was hard for Anna to concentrate on her work. Gibraltar School didn't seem so friendly anymore. And Anna was beginning to feel more weird than special.

Whenever Miss Crystal called on Chocolate, Anna forgot to answer. Besides, Anna was getting tired of her new name! It was hard enough getting used to a new school. Anna wasn't sure she wanted to get used to a new name, too.

Anna was also getting tired of her fancy

outfit. Her jewelry was noisy and jangly and scraped over the paper when she wrote.

Her necklace dragged in her spaghetti during lunch. Anna noticed it before it touched Kimberly's blouse, and wiped it clean with her napkin. It was a lot of work being a Sabbath child, and you really had to think a lot about being neat.

Then, in the art room, Anna reached for the brown paint and her bracelet got caught on the edge of the jar. She tried to shake it loose, but the paint jar bounced up and fell over, splattering brown paint all over Anna.

All the children were laughing at her! One girl said, "Now I know why they call you Chocolate!"

Stupid name! thought Anna. Stupid bracelet! Stupid everything! Anna had to squeeze her eyes shut to keep from crying.

Anna looked down at herself. There were ugly brown splotches all over, and the biggest ones were on Kimberly's lace blouse! Anna dipped a paper towel in the rinse water she'd been using to paint with. Then she rubbed at the brown spots with the towel. But the brown just spread into wider circles and now, mixed in with the brown, there were streaks of a horrible grayish color—the color of the rinse water. Anna rubbed in white chalk, to try to cover up the streaks of color. It looked worse than ever! Kimberly's good lace blouse was splotched and swirled, and it had gummy chalk on top of that.

Anna felt clumsy and stupid. She felt like a woe child. Now she would never make friends, not as just plain Anna, and certainly not as dumb, clumsy Chocolate.

"Good-bye . . . Chocolate," said Miss Crystal as Anna got ready to go home.

"Good-bye," said Anna. She felt the whole class watching her as she put her rain slicker over the whole, horrible mess.

Anna walked to the bus quickly and chose a seat in back. She saved a place for Kimberly, although she thought that Kimberly would surely have a friend to sit with by now.

Kimberly got on the bus alone. She looked around and saw Anna.

"I saved the seat for you," said Anna, scooting over so Kimberly could sit down.

"Thanks," said Kimberly, and took Anna's hand.

Kimberly really is nice, Anna thought. Anna was sorry she'd worn Kimberly's blouse. She felt as if the stain on Kimberly's blouse was burning a hole through her slicker, making a mark on the outside where everyone could see.

Kimberly used her key to open the door. Daddy was at the newspaper and Mom was working in the bookmobile. Anna was grateful she wouldn't have to look at either one of them. She didn't want to look at their faces when they asked about her day. They would expect her to say she had a wonderful day and made many new friends.

Anna rushed to her bedroom ahead of Kimberly. She closed the door quickly and took off her rain slicker and the stained and gummy blouse. She bunched up the blouse and hid it under the dresser, where she hoped Kimberly would never find it.

5

In Trouble Everywhere

"Where's my lace blouse?" asked Kimberly
the next morning. "I want to wear it." She
flung the hangers aside as she looked in the
back of the closet. "That's funny. I'm sure it
was here yesterday."

Kimberly's voice was muffled, as it came
floating to Anna from the back of the closet.
"Anna, do you know where my lace blouse
is?"

Anna didn't want to lie, so she just didn't
answer.

Kimberly kept looking. She looked under the beds, and behind the door. She looked on the bookshelf and inside the dresser. When Kimberly got on her knees to look under the dresser, Anna ran to the bathroom to brush her teeth. She looked at herself in the mirror. She saw a pale face with large, dark eyes. It was a face that was in trouble.

"*EEEeeek!*" shrieked Kimberly, from the bedroom. "My blouse! My best blouse! Mother!" Kimberly cried, her feet thundering down the stairs. "Look what Anna did to my blouse!"

"Anna!" called Mom in an angry voice.

Anna quickly squirted toothpaste onto her toothbrush and began humming loudly.

"Anna!" called Mom, louder.

Anna walked downstairs, brushing her teeth like crazy.

"Mmmyes?" she said, her mouth full of toothpaste.

Mom was standing at the kitchen counter. She was holding Kimberly's stained, gummy blouse with the tips of her fingers, like she didn't want to touch it.

"Anna," said Mom, "are you responsible for this?"

"Yes," said Anna, sorrowfully.

"Anna!" yelled Mom. "You had no right to take Kimberly's blouse without asking her! And now you've ruined a lovely blouse—Kimberly's favorite! These things cost money, Anna."

Anna knew she was supposed to say something, but what could she say? It was all true.

"What are we going to do with you, Anna? Sometimes you're so irresponsible! You just don't think."

Anna's face felt like it was burning up.

"Anna, say something!" Mom said, loudly.

But Anna didn't say anything. She couldn't.

"Anna Els Skoggen! I'm furious! What am I going to do with you?"

Anna swallowed her mouthful of toothpaste. "Punish me?" she asked quietly.

"Yes," said Mom. "I am. You're going to have to pay for Kimberly's blouse with your own money. It will take a long time to save that much money. Maybe then you'll learn to think before you do something. Maybe then

you'll learn to respect other people's prop-
erty."

"Okay," said Anna. "I'm sorry." And she
was. Anna was sorry she'd taken Kimberly's
blouse, and she was sorry she'd ruined it. Mom
didn't get angry very often. It was a big deal
when she did.

Now I'm in trouble everywhere, thought
Anna miserably. Mom and Kimberly are angry
because I ruined Kimberly's blouse. Everyone
at school thinks I'm clumsy and weird. Anna
wondered if there was anyone in the whole
world who didn't think she was terrible.

Later that day, at morning recess, Anna
looked longingly at all the children playing
with their friends. Some were playing four-
square. Some were playing jump rope and some
were playing run-away-from-the-boys. But
every single one of them was playing with
someone.

No one looked at Anna. No one said, "Anna,
come and play four-square with me." Or, "Anna,
let's jump rope." They wouldn't call her Anna,
anyway, thought Anna! They would call her

Chocolate. Whatever made her say her nick-name was Chocolate?

Anna stood like a movie star—with her toe pointed and her hand on her hip—but still no one noticed her. It wasn't the same without a fancy outfit. When Anna acted like a Sabbath child, she spilled things and jangled like a garbage truck. But when Anna acted like herself, no one noticed her. How Anna wished she were bonny and blithe and good and gay. How she wished she were special.

Anna walked to the edge of the third-grade playground. Third graders were supposed to stay on the blacktop. They were supposed to stay between the two little walls that jutted out from the corners of the building and not go on the other side.

Anna looked around the little wall. There was a cozy little corner. It seemed so secret in there! This was a place between the third-grade playground and the fourth-grade playground. Anna felt like she belonged in an in-between place like this. She decided to hide there. She snuck behind the wall. Anna crouched down low, with her knees pointing up and her chin resting on her knees. From down there she couldn't see the other children and they couldn't see her. This in-between land was hers and no one else's!

When the bell rang, Anna felt ready to face the rest of the day. If anything was terrible, she could just think about her secret place. So she thought about her secret place when Miss Crystal called, "Chocolate," and she forgot to answer. She thought about her secret place when the kids chose spelling teams and she was the last one picked. She thought about her secret place when the whole class drew pictures of their summer vacation and she became homesick.

At afternoon recess, Anna was anxious to get to her secret place and not see the faces of all the children who were not her friends.

Anna walked toward the edge of the playground, her fists bunched up against the unfairness of being a woe child. As she walked, she stomped on all the cracks in the blacktop that she could. It took a long time because there were a lot of cracks. She lingered on the third-grade side of the wall thinking about how great her secret place was going to be. Anna turned the corner slowly.

There, on the other side was another kid. An invader! How dare this kid hog Anna's secret spot! Besides, third graders weren't supposed to be here.

Anna couldn't even tell if it was a boy or a girl. It was wearing a Green Bay Packers hat and a Brewers jacket. When the kid turned its head, Anna saw a long braid snaking down its back. A girl, sniffed Anna. A girl in boy's clothes. Anna didn't say anything for a long time. She was waiting for the girl to say something first.

After a while, Anna gave in. "Third graders aren't supposed to be here."

The girl didn't say anything.

"Third graders," said Anna, louder and braver, "aren't supposed to be here."

"I know," said the girl, "but I'm not a third grader."

That explains it, thought Anna!

"Then why are you outside during third-grade recess?" asked Anna.

"Because," said the girl, slowly, looking down at the blacktop. "I, uh . . . well. . . ," she said, finally, "it's a long, long, *long* story."

Ha! Anna knew exactly what that meant. The girl couldn't think of anything to say because she wasn't telling the truth.

"I think you really are a third grader," said Anna, glad to have caught this invader in a lie.

"You're right. I am," said the girl, beginning to smile.

Anna felt a smile begin to tickle at the corners of her mouth. It stretched out slowly as it occurred to Anna that this girl was hiding, too.

"I'm Beth," said the girl, "but you can call me Bethie."

"I'm Anna," said Anna. "And you can call me Anna."

"But aren't you Chocolate?" asked Bethie.

"Well . . ." said Anna, giving herself time to think. "It's a long, long, *long* story."

Bethie's smile grew broader. She seemed to know exactly what Anna meant.

After recess, Anna and Bethie walked into

the classroom together. Miss Crystal looked up from the papers she was stapling and winked at the two girls.

"Hello, Chocolate," she said to Anna. "It looks as though you've had a nice recess."

"Yes," said Anna, "I did." Anna looked around the classroom. She was surprised to find several children looking at her. She was even more surprised when several of them said hi. Maybe they didn't hate her, after all. Maybe Gibraltar School wasn't that bad.

Someone poked Anna's back. She turned around and saw that the boy behind her was holding a note that had been folded many times. Anna turned back to the front and snuck her hand behind her back to grab the note. Then she opened her desk and pretended to look for something while she read the note.

The note said:

Anna,
   Let's wear the same clothes tomorrow.
OK?

                                   Your friend,
                                   Bethie

Anna put the note on top of her plastic bag of flies and wrote back:

Dear Bethie,

OK

Your friend,
Anna

Anna watched the note go from Collin to Kirsten to Elsa to Bethie. When Bethie got Anna's note, she opened her desk to read it.

Anna thought about what she and Bethie would wear tomorrow, and how everyone would know they were friends because they were wearing the same clothes.

After the bell rang, they talked about what they would wear.

"It has to be jeans," said Bethie, slinging her backpack over her shoulder. "That's all I have."

"Okay," she said. "And how about sweat-shirts?" She was sure Bethie would have sweatshirts.

"Yes!" cried Bethie. "I have lots. Green, red, and a gray one with the Roadrunner on it."

"Me, too," said Anna. "I have a Roadrunner sweatshirt, too!" Anna was sure it was a good sign to have the same kind of sweatshirts. She and Bethie were meant to be friends.

As Bethie and Anna were walking out of the classroom together, Miss Crystal called out, "Chocolate!"

Anna walked up to Miss Crystal's desk.

"Yes, Miss Crystal?" she said.

"Chocolate, I've been calling you a long time. I wonder, do you have a hearing problem?"

"No," said Anna. "I just, you know, daydream a little."

"Dreaming can be wonderful," said Miss Crystal. "But you have to learn to listen during class and dream at other times."

"I will," promised Anna.

"I have a note for you to take home to your parents," said Miss Crystal, and handed Anna a piece of paper.

"Thank you," said Anna, staring at the note.

Bethie had been waiting in the hall for Anna. "What does it say?" she asked.

"I don't know," said Anna, feeling the note get hot in her hand.

Anna waved good-bye to Bethie as she got on the bus. She thought about the note. Maybe it was about the paint disaster yesterday. Maybe it said she was a problem child. Maybe it said she had a hearing problem and should be tested. Or maybe it said she was the finest student Miss Crystal had ever had. Maybe it even said she showed signs of being gifted in the arts.

The note was taped shut, so Anna couldn't peek. The tape was stuck tightly, so she couldn't peel it off. The writing was in light-colored pencil, so she couldn't read it when she held it up to the light.

6

Luxury Day

Anna waited on the porch steps for Daddy to come home. She waited for a long time before she heard the little blue car coming down the street. "Daddy!" she cried, flinging herself at him. Daddy closed the car door with one hand, holding Anna with the other. They walked together up the porch stairs. "Did you have a nice day, Anna?" he asked.

"Yes," said Anna, "I did. I made a friend today and we're going to wear the same clothes tomorrow."

"You must be an individual, Anna—a leader," said Daddy, closing the front door. "Never follow the crowd."

Daddy didn't understand about best friends.

In the kitchen, Daddy poured two glasses of milk, one for himself and one for Anna.

Anna held the sweaty note out to Daddy.

"What do we have here?" asked Daddy, setting his milk glass on the counter. He slit the tape open and unfolded the note.

Anna had to stand on her toes to see over Daddy's shoulder. The note said:

> *Dear Mr. and Mrs. Skoggen:*
> *I enjoy having your daughter, Chocolate, in my class. She seems to be adjusting well to her new school.*
>
> > *Yours,*
> > *Miss Crystal*

"Chocolate?" asked Daddy, looking up from the note.

Anna examined her thumb knuckle closely.

"There must have been a mix-up and you were handed the wrong note," said Daddy, running his fingers through his school-paste hair. "I'll call Miss Crystal and tell her about the mix-up."

Just then Anna noticed Kimberly standing in the doorway, watching.

"Kimberly," she shouted. "You get out of here!" She felt she would die if Kimberly heard about the stupid thing she had done.

Kimberly moved away from the doorway, but Anna could hear her breathing on the other side.

"Kimberly Marie," said Daddy to the empty doorway. "I know you're still there. Anna and I are having a discussion and we don't need your assistance."

Kimberly's breathing stopped. She was either gone or dead.

"Now," said Daddy, "let's get to the bottom of this."

Anna jiggled while Daddy looked up Miss Crystal's name in the phone book. She cleaned her fingernails while Daddy wrote the number on a piece of paper. She snapped and unsnapped her jeans while Daddy picked up the phone.

"I'm Chocolate," Anna mumbled.

Daddy didn't hear her. He started dialing.

Anna said, more loudly, "I am Chocolate."

Click. Daddy put the phone back on the hook.

Anna said, "They call me Chocolate at school."

Daddy pulled out a chair for Anna to sit down.

"Why would anyone call you Chocolate?"

"Because I told them to call me Chocolate," said Anna.

Daddy's eyebrows squeezed together. "Why?" he asked.

Anna sighed. She was going to have to explain the whole thing.

"I wanted to be a Sabbath child," she said in one breath, "like in the poem. I wanted to be bonny and blithe and good and gay, like Kimberly. So I dressed up fancy on the first day of school. That's why I wore my rain slicker, so you wouldn't notice my new look."

"Anna, you must try to be yourself," Daddy said. "You mustn't try to be something you're not. But, all that aside, I still don't understand how you became known as Chocolate."

74

"Because," Anna said, "when Miss Crystal called out 'Anna Skoggen,' I said, 'Call me Chocolate.' I'm not sure why I said that," said Anna, with a shaky voice. "It sounded good when I said it. Everybody likes chocolate, and I wanted everybody to like me. But then I spilled paint on Kimberly's blouse, and everybody laughed!"

Anna felt her neck and eyes get hot. She felt tears fill up her eyes and spill out, dripping down her cheek. Daddy reached out for Anna and lifted her onto his lap.

"What a terrible, terrible day," he said.

Daddy wrapped his long arms around Anna and held her tightly. It felt good to cry into Daddy's chest and feel his long arms wrapped around her. Daddy didn't let go until Anna stopped crying. Then he wrote a note to Miss Crystal:

> Dear Miss Crystal,
> We're happy that our daughter is ad-justing to her new school. However, we would like you to call our daughter Anna, and not Chocolate. Chocolate is an old nickname and

isn't appropriate for a girl as grown up as
our daughter Anna.

> *Yours,*
> *Paul Skoggen*

Anna's eyes felt clean and her chest felt lighter. Now at least she wouldn't be stuck with that stupid nickname anymore.

Anna heard the screen door slam. Mom was home from her job at the bookmobile. She heard the keys jangle as Mom laid them on the hall table. Mom, wearing soft-soled shoes, walked soundlessly to the kitchen.

"Hello, dear," she said to Daddy as she slid an armload of books onto the counter. "I brought home some books for the family—yours is on top."

Daddy picked up his book and started paging through it. Mom sat down at the table and slipped off her shoes and rubbed her feet.

"Anna," she said, holding out her arms for a hug. "How was your day today?"

"Just fine, Mom," Anna said.

Anna hugged Mom and looked at Daddy. Over Mom's shoulder she mouthed the words,

"Don't tell Mom." Daddy hesitated a minute, and then slid the notes into his book.

"I made a new friend, her name is Bethie," said Anna, "and we're going to wear the same clothes tomorrow."

Daddy started to say, "Anna, be yourself." But Mom said, "How wonderful! That will show everyone you're friends. I remember when my best friend Judy and I wore matching outfits. In fact, one year we bought exactly the same dress. Our best-friend dresses were red plaid with black sashes."

Anna was glad to hear she was doing the same kind of thing Mom had done as a girl.

Mom rubbed the back of her neck.

"Do you have a headache, Helen?" asked Daddy.

"Yes," said Mom. "The bookmobile is a lot of work. I don't know the roads very well yet, and I don't know the people at the schools. There's so much to learn."

Anna wanted to make Mom feel better. "Then I'll give you and Daddy a luxury day!" cried Anna, bouncing up and down. "I'll give you a backrub and make the whole dinner and do all the dishes."

"That's a lot of work," said Mom. "Perhaps we should do it together."

"No, Mom," said Kimberly, walking in the kitchen. "I'll help Anna. You just relax."

"Oh, thank you, Kimberly. You're so sweet!"

Mom walked slowly into the living room with Daddy. Anna heard her sink into the big leather chair. She heard the newspaper rustle.

Thwap! Anna threw the ground meat into a bowl. "You don't have to help," she said to Kimberly. "I can do it myself."

Anna wanted to do something nice for Mom all by herself. Now Kimberly was butting in. Anna smashed an egg on the side of the bowl and added it to the meat. Some of the egg-shells slid in, flecking the meat mixture with hard little pieces of white. Anna hoped Kimberly would get the shells in her piece of meat-loaf. She picked up an onion and started to peel it. Her eyes were red and runny, so she didn't see Kimberly reach over. "Here, I'll do it," Kimberly said, grabbing the onion.

"I can do it," said Anna, grabbing it back.

"Suit yourself," said Kimberly. Kimberly chopped celery while Anna peeled the onion. Kimberly added spices to the meat while Anna peeled the onion. Kimberly adjusted the oven temperature and cubed the bread. Kimberly put frozen corn into a pan. All while Anna peeled the onion.

At dinner Mom said, "This is delicious! It's the best meal I've ever had!"

After dinner Anna and Kimberly did dishes. Kimberly said she would wash, to make sure the dishes were clean. As if Anna would have left them dirty! Still, Anna felt good because she'd given a luxury day to Mom.

She was happy it was her idea. Kimberly was just a copycat. And she was happy to be going to school tomorrow as Anna instead of Chocolate.

The next day, Anna handed Daddy's note to Miss Crystal. Miss Crystal read the note with a serious face.

"Very well," she said, finally. "I'll call you Anna."

Anna felt relieved as she walked to her seat. She sat at her desk, looking around the class- room. Everyone was talking!

Anna liked the noisy buzz in the classroom. Bethie rushed in, dropped a book, picked it up. When she saw Anna, she grinned. They looked like twins, except for Anna's red hair and Bethie's long braid!

Miss Crystal raised her hand to get the attention of the class. The buzzing softened and finally stopped.

"Children," said Miss Crystal, "the third-grade class is going to put on a play. The play is called *Golden Wishes*. There are seven parts in the play, which are listed here." Miss Crystal handed everyone a sheet of paper.

LILAH 1: A golden-haired princess with a musical voice.

LILAH 2: The grown-up Lilah.

JOSEPH: Lilah's friend. A poor lad who lives near the castle.

THE KING: Lilah's father.

THE SPINNING WITCH: The wicked witch who tries to influence Lilah.

81

POT OF GOLD: Lilah's first wish.
MISS HAPPINESS: Lilah's second wish.

Anna read the list and quickly decided on her part—The Spinning Witch. It would be fun to be wicked! And Anna knew just how to make her voice crackly and old like a witch. She raised her hand and waved it until Miss Crystal said, "Yes, Anna?"

"May I be The Spinning Witch?" asked Anna.

"All of you will have a chance to try out for the parts you want. We'll have tryouts, just like in a real play. After tryouts I'll select the best actor or actress for the part.

Stephanie Bolter raised her hand. Stephanie Bolter, Anna knew, wanted to be Lilah 1. She had a golden voice and looked like a princess. "Miss Crystal, when will you hold tryouts?"

"We'll have the tryouts Monday morning. I'll hand out copies of the play after school today, so you can practice reading the part you want."

At lunch recess, Bethie and Anna walked

arm in arm and talked about the play.

"What do you want to be?" asked Anna.

"The Pot of Gold," said Bethie. "I'd like to be rich. What do you want to be?"

"The Spinning Witch," said Anna. "I want to be wicked and have a witchy voice. *Nye-he-he!*" cackled Anna, spinning around.

"Money money money," shouted Bethie, rubbing her hands together greedily.

The two friends raced across the playground cackling and shouting. Then they stretched out on the warm blacktop and looked up at the sky, watching the sea gulls dive and float. There was a twinkle in the sky, and Anna thought it might be a star. She said, "Star light, star bright, first star I see tonight . . ."

"Does it count if you wish on a star in the daytime?" asked Bethie.

"Yes," said Anna, "it probably counts double because daytime stars are so rare."

"Then you'd better say 'first star I see today.'"

"Okay. Star light, star bright, first star I see today, I wish I might, I wish I may have the wish I wish today."

"Good," said Bethie, nodding.

Anna made her wish silently, because you can't wish a wish out loud or it won't come true. Anna wished she would be The Spinning Witch. Then she would be special.

7

Blood Sisters

Anna and Bethie practiced all week long for
Golden Wishes. Now it was Saturday, and they
were at the Sweet Scoop Ice Cream Shoppe.
The owner, Mrs. Michaels, let special cus-
tomers create their own sundaes. Today she
was going to help Bethie and Anna make theirs.

"One scoop of pistachio," ordered Bethie.

"And one scoop of maple," said Anna. Mrs.
Michaels dug deeply into the ice cream tubs.
She curled one scoop of pistachio and then

one scoop of maple around her spoon and nudged them into a dish.

"Pineapple sauce," said Anna.

"And marshmallow cream," said Bethie. Mrs. Michaels spooned the pineapple sauce and marshmallow cream onto the ice cream.

"Now bananas," Anna said. She knelt up on the stool to see Mrs. Michaels slice the bananas and slide them next to the ice cream.

"Chopped nuts," said Bethie. Mrs. Michaels sprinkled nuts on top.

"Whipped cream," said Anna. Mrs. Michaels squirted.

"More . . . " said Bethie.

"More . . . " said Anna. Mrs. Michaels mounded the whipped cream high.

"And a dab of chocolate," said Anna. Mrs. Michaels drizzled chocolate, and added two maraschino cherries for good measure. "This is a masterpiece," Mrs. Michaels said. "We'll call it a Beth-Anna Split."

Bethie and Anna carried their sundae to a booth. "What do you want to do today?" asked Anna.

"I don't know. What do you want to do?"

"I don't know.'"

"Do you want to play checkers?" asked Anna.

"No," said Bethie. "Let's do something exciting." Bethie's long braid dropped into the whipped cream and chocolate. She flipped it to her back, where it left a brown stain on her sweatshirt.

"We can pretend the widow's walk is a ship— the ship *Margway*." Margway sounded exotic and dangerous to Anna.

"No . . . " said Bethie. "Let's think of something more exciting." Bethie's long braid slid over her shoulder and into the sticky, melted remains of the Beth-Anna Split. "This stupid braid," she said. "I wish I could get rid of it!"

"Your hair?" said Anna.

"Yes," said Bethie.

Anna looked at Bethie, her eyes dancing, and waited for Bethie to guess.

"You mean . . . ?" asked Bethie, making a scissors motion with her fingers across the middle of the gooey braid.

Anna nodded.

"I'll cut mine if you cut yours."

"Okay!" cried Anna. They put their money

on the table and hurried outside. They walked down the street close together, heads bent toward each other.

"Tryouts are Monday," said Anna.

"And we really should look good for tryouts," said Bethie.

"All actresses have their hair done before tryouts."

They walked home so fast their feet hardly touched the sidewalk.

"Where are the scissors?" asked Bethie.

"Here," said Anna, digging into Mom's sewing basket. "Mom said never never use this on paper, but she didn't say never never use this on hair."

Bethie and Anna took the scissors into the upstairs bathroom and locked the door.

"First I'll be the beautician," said Anna, "and you be the customer." Anna pinned two towels to Bethie, like in a beauty parlor.

"Have you ever cut anyone's hair before?" asked Bethie.

"Millions of times," said Anna. Anna had cut hair before, but it was only dolls' hair.

Bethie's eyes were large and round. She

didn't look very happy. Maybe she didn't really want to get her hair cut.

"Are you sure you want your hair cut, Bethie?" asked Anna.

Bethie slowly drew the braid from her back and looked at the dried ice cream with bits of sticky chocolate on the end. "Go ahead," she said.

Anna tried to cut the braid in one large *snip*, but it was too thick. She unbraided Bethie's hair and found it cut quite easily that way. *Snip-snip. Snip-snip-snap.* The braid was off.

"Let me do the rest," said Bethie, reaching for the scissors. Bethie cut her bangs very, very short. She cut the sides short, too. She couldn't reach the back very well, so she let Anna do that. Then she examined herself in the mirror, angling her head this way and that.

"It will look better after it's washed," Anna said. "Now me." She cut away at her own hair. She'd admired the shaggy style she saw on a rock star once, and decided to cut her hair that way. *Snip-snip.* Anna angled the scissors up into her hair, snipping at the ends so they looked shaggy.

Snip-snip. Large chunks of Anna's hair dropped to the ground. When she was done, she looked at herself in the mirror. She didn't look very much like the picture of the rock star.

"It will look better after it's washed," Bethie said. "What will we do next?"

Bethie and Anna looked around the bathroom for more ways to be beautiful. First they put Ravishing Red polish on their fingernails and added a few spritzes of Evening in Calcutta perfume. Then they decided to shave their legs.

Swooooish. The cream squirted out in creamy white piles, like Mrs. Michaels' whipped cream. Squirting was even more fun than shaving.

"More," said Bethie, mounding the cream higher.

"More," said Anna, squirting out more.

They rested their legs on the toilet lid, the way they'd seen their mothers do. Then they got the razor. They knew the razor was sharp, and they had to be very careful. Slowly they drew the razor through the cream, cutting off the hair underneath. There was so much cream, though, that it was hard to tell just where they were shaving. Wet gobs of white cream splatted to the floor. When the cream was mostly shaved off. Bethie and Anna were surprised to see traces of bloody streaks on their legs.

"Oh," said Bethie. "I didn't know we were cutting our skin."

"Me, either. But—no pain, no gain." Anna had heard her father say that many times. She just wished there had been a little less pain.

"Let's be blood sisters, like Indians," said Bethie, wiping some pink shaving cream onto her finger and mixing it with Anna's.

"Forever and ever," said Anna, swelling with love for her best friend.

Knock knock knock.

"Who's there?" asked Anna.

"It's me. Kimberly. What are you doing in there?"

"Nothing," said Anna, wetting down the sticking-out parts of her hair.

"You've been in there a long time and I need to use the bathroom," said Kimberly. "If you don't let me in, I'll call Mom."

Anna opened the door and hid behind it.

The perfumed explosion of Evening in Calcutta reached Kimberly. "Pew!" she said. She looked at the stained white towels. She looked at the floor, mounded with hair clippings. Then she looked behind the door.

"Anna!" cried Kimberly. Her eyes moved from Anna's hair to her fingernails to her legs. She looked at Bethie. "Your braid!"

The three stared into the bathroom mirror. What a sight! Bethie's bangs and sides were nearly shaved. The back of her hair was uneven. Anna's hair was wet and chopped up. Anna looked like a wet chicken that was going bald!

"You've really done it this time!" said Kimberly.

"It will look better when it's washed," said Bethie.

"Well, it won't look good enough," said Kimberly.

"And this mess! We've got to clean it up," Kimberly said, gathering up the towels. Anna mopped the floor with a washcloth, and Bethie cleaned up the shaving cream and hair clippings.

"Now your hair," said Kimberly. Kimberly evened up the back of Bethie's hair a little. It looked a little better. "Anna, I can't fix your hair—it's too short," she said. "You're just going to have to wait for it to grow out."

"That's okay," said Anna, feeling her throat get thick with panic. What if she looked too freaky to be in the play? And what would Mom say when she saw Anna's hair? She would be angry with Anna. Maybe Mom would be as angry as she had been with the blouse. Maybe angrier!

"Come on," said Kimberly as she watched Anna's frightened face. "I'll go with you to tell Mom."

They said good-bye to Bethie, who felt it was bad enough to face *one* angry mother. Kimberly put her arm around Anna's shoulder and they walked into the living room.

Mom was playing the piano. She was playing a dancing kind of song, light and quick. *Dee-de-dum. Dee-de-dum.* Mom stared at the white wall over the piano, weaving her body in time to the music. *Dee-de-dum. Dee-de-dum.* Kimberly and Anna stood next to Mom.

94

They were waiting for her to notice them. *Dum!* She noticed! Mom's hands slid off the keyboard as she stared at Anna's hair. Kimberly held Anna's shoulder tightly.

"Anna," cried Mom, sadly. She reached out and smoothed down Anna's spiky hair. "Oh, dear! My poor baby!"

Anna had thought Mom would get angry. She hadn't thought Mom would feel sorry for her! Feeling sorry was worse! Once again, Anna had been a disappointment to her mother.

8

Tryouts

Anna jammed a Green Bay Packers hat down over her hair as she watched Mom standing with her arm around Kimberly. Kimberly didn't ride the bus with Anna that morning because she had a dental appointment. Anna wished she hadn't disappointed Mom again. She wished she were the one—the beautiful one with silky hair—under Mom's arm.

Anna had hoped she'd be The Spinning Witch. She had the whole thing planned. She would wear a wonderful costume with a pointed

96

hat and a long black skirt that swooshed when she walked. She would say her lines so creatively—with so much drama—that everyone would know she was a born actress. How proud Mom would be! Her beloved Anna, the actress in the family.

And now, no matter how well she read her part, she'd never get to be The Spinning Witch. All the children would laugh at her when they saw her hair. Miss Crystal would not let a freaky girl act in the play!

Anna wanted to wear her hat inside the school, but Miss Crystal said, "Anna, hats belong on the coat rack. You know that."

Slowly, Anna walked to the coat rack. She put the hat on the shelf and waited for a minute before walking back inside.

"Holy cow!" cried Collin. "Look at Anna's hair. It looks like it's shredded."

Anna felt like she was frozen to the floor. She couldn't make her feet move.

Stephanie-Bolter-with-golden-hair laughed politely behind her hand. Some of the others laughed, but not very politely.

Anna wished she could walk through the

wall and into another world on the other side. There she would not do stupid things and everyone would like her. In the other world, no one would be laughing at her.

Bethie, whose hair looked terrible too, managed a small smile for Anna.

Anna's feet finally started to move. As she walked to her desk, Miss Crystal said, "Why, Anna! I'll bet you're trying out for the part of The Spinning Witch. You must have fussed with your hair for hours to get it to look like that. You're certainly a dedicated actress."

Anna hadn't thought of that. Her hair was perfect for The Spinning Witch! Anna sat down. She was a dedicated actress! Anna and Bethie smiled at each other.

"I don't believe we'll get any work done until we hold tryouts," said Miss Crystal. "I can see we have some very eager actresses."

Anna sat up very tall, proud to be an actress.

Miss Crystal moved some furniture aside in the front of the classroom to make room for the actors.

The first tryouts were for Lilah 1. Several

girls tried out for this part, but Stephanie Bolter got the role. Anna knew she would.

Tryouts for Lilah 2 were next. Kirsten Olafson got that part because she was the tallest.

Lief Johnson got the part of Joseph. He didn't really want to be Joseph (nobody did); he wanted to be The King.

"But Lief," Miss Crystal said, "this part needs to be played by someone very strong and powerful, and I think you are the boy to do it." Lief agreed.

The Pot of Gold tryouts were next. Two boys and two girls tried out for this part, but Bethie was the best. She sounded so rich and greedy when she read that Anna was sure she'd get the part.

"You read with real enthusiasm, Bethie," said Miss Crystal. "You have the part."

The King tryouts took a long time and gave Anna a chance to get nervous. The Spinning Witch was next. How many girls would try out for The Spinning Witch? What if Anna had to go first, and everyone else used Anna's idea for a creaky voice? What if they laughed at her? What if someone else got the part?

"And now," said Miss Crystal, "The Spinning Witch."

Three girls walked to the front of the class, including Anna. Her hands were cold and sweaty.

First, Clair Peters read. She read perfectly, without any mistakes. But she sounded like Clair Peters, not a witch. Next, Estelle Tolan. Estelle stumbled on the words. Maybe she didn't practice. Maybe she was just nervous. Anna was nervous too! What if she stumbled on the words, like Estelle Tolan?

"Anna!" Anna looked up. "It's your turn," said Miss Crystal.

Anna unraveled the tightly rolled, sweaty script she'd been clutching. She cleared her throat and read in a slightly creaky voice.

"Lilah. Lilah! Let me help you choose the right wish. You won't be sorry."

No one was laughing at Anna. Miss Crystal, in fact, smiled. That encouraged Anna. She hunched over like a witch and continued reading in a very crackly, old voice.

"Choose wealth! Choose jewels! Choose

gold! You'll be the richest princess in the kingdom!"

Anna held a finger to the sky and cackled *"Nye-he-he-he,"* in a wicked, witchy laugh. The laugh wasn't part of the script, but Anna felt it belonged. When she finished reading, she looked up at Miss Crystal. "Anna!" said Miss Crystal. "That was wonderful. You really are an actress!"

The whole class applauded. Collin whistled.

Anna smiled the happy smile of a girl who is proud of herself. Her stomach felt shimmery and tickly, and it became difficult to hold still. She felt so good!

"Anna," announced Miss Crystal, "you'll be our Spinning Witch."

The next week went by much too quickly for Anna, who enjoyed all the attention. The whole class looked forward to the time Anna came on stage and laughed her wicked, witchy laugh.

Then, on Wednesday she said, "I think smoke would make the play look spookier."

"Yeah," said Collin.

"It would set off the fire alarm," said Stephanie Bolter.

Anna said, "No, it wouldn't. I know just how to do it! You put water on dry ice and it will look like smoke."

"Why, Anna! That's a wonderful idea," said Miss Crystal.

Anna had other ideas, too, for lighting—flashing a floodlight on and off for bolts of lightning—and costumes—spraying gold paint on Bethie's leotards so she would sparkle like real gold. On Thursday, Anna had the best idea of all. "I think The Spinning Witch should fly onto the stage!"

"Fly?" said Stephanie Bolter, her eyebrows shooting up into her forehead.

Miss Crystal thought it was a great idea. The janitor put together a pulley with the harness from gymnastics. They hooked Anna into it and she climbed up a tall ladder behind the stage. When Anna nodded to Collin, he opened the curtains a little. Then she jumped off the ladder and flew!

Anna felt like a sea gull! It was wonderful!

103

Flying was so much fun, she wanted to keep practicing her entrance.

After Anna had flown onto the stage seven times, Miss Crystal said, "I think you've got it down now, Anna."

"Yes," Anna had to agree. The flying, the smoke, the costumes, her witchy laugh— everything was perfect! Now she would really be a star!

9

"Break A Leg"

Anna and Kimberly were sitting at the kitchen table. "You don't need to practice again. As it is, you can say your lines forward, backward, or from the middle," Kimberly said. "In fact, *I* could say them forward, backward, or from the middle."

"Come on, Kimberly, this has to be perfect. Let's do it again. You be Lilah."

"Okay," said Kimberly, flipping over the cover of the play and beginning to read the first line. Kimberly read the lines for the other characters. Anna read her own. As always, Anna made no mistakes.

When she was through reading, she heard clapping. "Bravo!" cried Daddy from the kitchen doorway.

Anna grinned. "Are you coming to the play tomorrow?"

"Of course," he said, pouring milk into a mug. "I wouldn't miss it."

"Will you write an article about the play?" asked Anna, excitedly.

"A review," said Daddy. Daddy added the cocoa.

A real review, thought Anna. Like a famous play!

"We're so proud of you!" said Mom, walking over to Anna and hugging her.

Anna felt like she would burst! Finally, things were going her way.

"What do you think I should wear for the performance?" asked Mom. "I need to wear something appropriate for mother of the witch." Tapping her finger to her chin, she said, "So you're a witch and I'm your mother. Do you think that means I'm a witch, too?"

"Witches do run in the family," said Daddy with a serious face. Daddy seemed to be squeezing a smile back inside. "But, of course," he added, "it only runs on the female side. Mother to daughter, you know."

Mom took the broom out of the closet and pretended to sweep Daddy away. "Why, Paul! We may just turn you into a frog. Isn't that right, Anna?"

"Nye-he-he-he-he!" cackled Anna in a blood-chilling laugh.

"Nye-he-he-he-he!" cackled Mom. Mom's laugh was pretty good, but not as good as Anna's.

Anna carried her and Kimberly's cocoa to their room. Kimberly was already in bed, propped up on her pillows. She was sketching mauve fairies and unicorns in a deep, green forest.

"Here, Kimberly," said Anna, handing Kimberly her cocoa.

"Thanks, Anna. I'll bet you're excited about tomorrow." Kimberly's pencil danced over the page, leaving soft strokes of color behind it.

"Yes," said Anna, sipping her cocoa. It

seemed to Anna that when Kimberly sketched her hand was magic. Anna wished she had magic in her hand, too.

Maybe the play was just the beginning of magic for Anna. Maybe after tomorrow other wonderful things would happen. Maybe she would learn to draw. Maybe she would fill the bookshelf with trophies. Anna stuck her finger into her empty mug to scrape up the chocolate at the bottom. She sucked her finger clean and turned out the light.

Anna looked out of the moon window. I'll be looking at this same sky tomorrow, she thought. But tomorrow everything will be different. Tomorrow I'll be a star!

Anna imagined how everyone would gasp when she flew onto the stage. She imagined how they would watch as she hobbled and cackled. She imagined the applause. Loud, rumbling applause coming like waves on the sand.

People would walk up to Kimberly and say, "You're so lucky to share a room with such a talented actress."

Kimberly would be jealous and say, "I was Student of the Week last month." But people wouldn't care. They would only want to talk about the famous Spinning Witch. Anna would be nice to Kimberly because she would know that Kimberly was jealous. Maybe she would give her the dead fly collection to keep on the bookshelf.

People would call up Mom and say, "You must be very proud of your beloved daughter Anna."

Mom would say, "Yes, I certainly am thrilled to be her mother."

At last Anna would be special! At last Mom and Daddy would be proud of her.

Anna woke up very early the next morning. She practiced her part for a while, then examined her dead fly collection. She crossed yesterday off the calendar, she adjusted the shade on the moon window. She checked out the cereals downstairs to see which one she would want to eat at breakfast. She shut herself inside the pantry and ate some cookies.

Anna opened the milk chute. It was cool outside now, and she was sure she could slide right through if she tried. But Anna didn't. Today it was not absolutely necessary to crawl through the milk chute, and Anna didn't want to be late for school. Not today. Finally, everyone came down for breakfast.

"This is the big day," announced Daddy.

"Break a leg, Anna," said Kimberly, pouring cereal into her bowl.

"What?" said Anna.

Kimberly laughed. "That's what you say to wish an actress good luck."

"Oh," said Anna, shaking her thin, freckled leg. She was glad she didn't really have to break it for good luck.

Mom cleared off the table while Kimberly left with Daddy. Daddy had to bring Kimberly back to the dentist.

Alone at the table, Anna stared at the air in front of her. She was imagining her spectacular entrance. Suddenly Mom looked at Anna. "You're not dressed! What have you been doing all this time? Finish your cereal and run upstairs and get dressed. You're late!"

Anna shoved the last bites of cereal into her mouth and ran up the stairs. Socks. Pants. Shoes. Anna was jamming her arms into her sweatshirt when she heard Mom call, "Hurry, Anna! The bus is here!"

What if she missed the bus? What if the bus left without her? What if they held the dress rehearsal without her?

The bus driver honked impatiently. The quickest way down was the tree. And this time it was absolutely necessary! Anna didn't even wait to tie her shoes before she ran to the widow's walk. She swung her leg over the railing, shoelaces dangling. The railing cracked dangerously, but Anna made it over safely.

Anna grabbed onto the first big branch and swung her leg down to reach the second, but felt only air. Anna grabbed for something to hold on to. Her hands scraped at the tree, tearing her nails and making her fingertips numb. She was falling too fast and she couldn't hold on.

Mom ran outside when she heard Anna yell.

There was Anna, The Spinning Witch, lying on the ground beneath the big tree. She was twisting and kicking in frustration and pain.

Tenderly, Mom laid Anna on the couch.

"I'm not hurt," cried Anna. "I have to go to school!"

Mom was feeling Anna's legs, head, and finally her arms.

"Ouch!" said Anna when Mom got to her left arm.

"It may be broken, Anna," said Mom.

"It's not!" cried Anna, fighting back tears. "It's not, it's not, it's not! It's just bruised and if I go to school I'll be all right. Take me right now or I'll miss the rehearsal! Please!"

"Anna," said Mom, gently, "we need to have your arm checked."

"No!" shouted Anna. Tears were beginning to fill her eyes, but she pushed them back inside. Anna didn't want Mom to see her cry.

The third grade would have the play without her and Anna wouldn't get to be The Spinning Witch! She wouldn't get to fly on the stage! She wouldn't get to spin and cackle! She wouldn't get to wear the costume! And worse, Anna wouldn't get to show Mom and Daddy what a talented actress she was!

Now Mom and Daddy would *never* be proud of Anna. They would *never* think that Anna was special. This was Anna's big chance, and now her chance was ruined. And her arm hurt! Anna had squeezed her bad feelings inside for so long that now they were pushing to get out.

Mom bent over Anna and said, "Anna, I have to make a few phone calls. Will you be all right for a few minutes?"

Anna nodded.

Mom began to dial, all the while watching Anna.

"Dr. Gritt?" she said. "Anna fell from a tree. I think her arm may be broken. Yes. Yes. We'll be there right away."

Then, "Miss Crystal, this is Helen Skoggen. I have some very bad news. Anna fell from a tree. It looks like her arm is broken. . . . Yes, I feel terrible, too. I know how important it was to Anna. . . . No, she can't very well fly with a broken arm, can she? No alternates?

114

Yes, I agree. It would be a shame not to hold the play. But who? . . . Miss Crystal," Mom said quickly, "I almost forgot. Kimberly knows all the lines and can fill in for Anna."

Kimberly!

It was bad enough that Anna couldn't be The Spinning Witch. But now Kimberly was going to do it instead. Kimberly was going to fly and do all the things Anna had dreamed about! Anna was so upset she couldn't breathe. She tried breathing deeply, but it wasn't working.

Mom rushed over to Anna with a paper bag and put it over Anna's mouth and nose. "Breathe slowly," Mom said. "This paper bag will help you take better breaths." All the while, Mom smoothed Anna's chopped-up hair with light, cool fingers. Mom waited until Anna was breathing more easily. Then she asked, "Do you think you can walk to the car? We need to see Dr. Gritt."

"Yes," Anna said.

Mom held the steering wheel so tight her knuckles were white.

I wanted to be a star! Anna thought. Everything was going to be different after today, and now everything's going to be the same. I'm still Anna the Woe Child. And Kimberly! Kimberly's going to be the star! Tears were choking Anna's throat, but still she would not let them out.

Mom parked the car and ran around to Anna's side. "Let me help you out, Anna," said Mom, reaching out to her.

"I can do it myself," said Anna, in a voice tight with tears. Mom reached out to Anna again, but Anna started walking toward the clinic door.

"Hello, Anna," said Dr. Gritt, washing his hands in the little sink in his office. "Your mother tells me you fell from a tree."

Anna didn't feel like talking, so she just nodded her head.

Dr. Gritt had soft, shy eyes like a puppy's. He had a nice smile and hair that was a little shaggy. He had several white, shiny scars on his chin. Anna thought he probably understood about climbing trees when it was ab-

116

solutely necessary. Dr. Gritt scooted along on his stool to get closer to Anna. His hands, still damp from washing, gently held Anna's hurt arm. "Broken." Dr. Gritt didn't say many words. The words he said were important ones.

"I'll send Anna to X ray," he said to Mom, "and then we'll fix her up."

Anna's X rays proved Dr. Gritt was right. Her arm was broken.

Mom held Anna while Dr. Gritt got ready to straighten her arm. "This will hurt, Anna," he said, "but I have to do it. I'm sorry."

Dr. Gritt's puppy eyes did look sorry. Anna was ready for a big hurt. I will not cry, she thought.

Crack! It hurt a little when Anna's arm snapped into place. But Anna couldn't squeeze her tears inside anymore. I don't know why I'm crying, she thought as she cried. It didn't hurt so much. But Anna wasn't crying about a broken arm. She was crying about being a woe child.

Anna cried into Mom's blouse as Dr. Gritt slid something onto Anna's arm that looked like a sock. He wrapped gooey gauze around it. It felt hot! Anna was beginning to feel sick to her stomach. She wanted to go home. Mom's voice and Dr. Gritt's voice seemed far away, like on the other side of a tunnel. The room turned gray and wobbly. Suddenly Anna felt very, very heavy, so heavy she couldn't stay awake. Anna fainted into Mom's arms.

Anna's arm throbbed with pain all day, but even that was a small thing compared to what she felt inside. Mom read to her, brought her hot cocoa, and fluffed her pillow, but nothing could comfort her. Tonight she would not be a star. Tonight Kimberly was going to take her part.

She watched the clock moving, getting closer to three-thirty, the time Kimberly would get home. Anna knew what would happen. Kimberly would fling open the door and blast inside, all sad and worried because Anna hadn't been in school. When Mom told her what happened she would say, "Poor thing!" Then, when Mom told her *she* would be The Spinning Witch, Kimberly would say, "Me? Oh, I don't think I could. But I suppose they need me." Then she would look at Anna with fake sadness.

At three-thirty the front door burst open, just as Anna knew it would. "Mom!" she heard Kimberly's voice from downstairs. "Miss Crystal told me Anna broke her arm!"

"Yes, she did." Mom whispered, like she was in a hospital. "She feels just awful, Kimberly, and so do I. Go on upstairs, honey. Maybe you . . ."

Anna put the pillow over her head. She didn't want to hear the rest. Too soon Anna's bedroom door opened. Kimberly rushed in and sat on the edge of Anna's bed. Anna glared at Kimberly's sorrowful face.

"Anna," she said, "I'm so sorry this happened. I know how much you wanted to be The Spinning Witch." Kimberly reached for Anna's good arm, but Anna pulled it away.

Then Mom came in and sat down beside Anna. "Kimberly, it would be such a shame to cancel the play. I told Miss Crystal that you knew Anna's part and you could be The Spinning Witch."

Anna waited for Kimberly to blush with pleasure. But instead, her face became very

119

white. Anna waited for her to make a weak protest and then say she'd play the part after all. But instead, Kimberly said nothing. Nothing at all.

10

This Time For Anna

Anna and Kimberly had been unusually quiet all afternoon. So Mom and Daddy had been chattering, trying to fill up the silence. Now, in the car on the way to the play, they continued.

"It's a lovely fall evening, Paul," said Mom.

"It will be winter soon," said Daddy. "I'd better order more wood for the fireplace."

"Yes, perhaps you should. There's nothing like a fire on a cold winter night."

"Right," said Daddy.

"Right," said Mom.

Mom turned on the radio. She fiddled with the tuner until she found a noisy rock station, not her usual choice.

The rock station pounded on while the Skoggens sat in silence.

At school, Anna got out of the car and walked alone toward the big front doors. Her feet were so heavy, she felt like she was walking in cement. Bright lights from inside were streaming onto the sidewalk. Anna could see a lot of people including Bethie, whose face was pressed against the window.

"Anna!" cried Bethie, swinging open the door and running to her friend. "Miss Crystal said you broke your arm!"

Anna angled her broken arm toward Bethie. The white cast looked bright and eerie under the streetlights.

"Does it hurt?" she asked.

"Yes," whispered Anna hoarsely.

"Is it true," Bethie said, face close to Anna's, "that *Kimberly* is going to be The Spinning Witch?"

"Yes," said Anna.

"Oh, Anna! How awful!" Bethie's sorrowful face was real, not fake, and Anna knew she understood. The two friends walked together in silence through the big orange doors and down the hall. They walked toward the gymnasium through the door that led behind the stage.

"Anna, it won't be the same without you," said Bethie.

Bethie picked up the pot costume and strapped it over her shoulders. "I won't even watch Kimberly. I'll close my eyes and then I'll imagine you on the stage, not Kimberly."

Miss Crystal was busy hooking up the pulley. She hurried down the ladder toward Anna. "I am so sorry! Your arm must really hurt!"

"Yes," said Anna. She was getting sick of talking about her arm.

"Help, Miss Crystal!" cried Lief Johnson. He was struggling with some of the scenery and Miss Crystal and Bethie went to help.

Just then Daddy came over to Anna and said, "Anna, I know you're very disappointed you won't be in this play. But if you can, I'd like you to help Kimberly from behind the stage. You may need to prompt her with lines."

Anna stared at Daddy. She couldn't believe he was asking her to help Kimberly. Didn't he know she could barely *look* at Kimberly, let alone help her? Helping Kimberly be a star was the absolute last thing Anna wanted to do. She wondered if this evening could possibly get worse. But when she thought of Kimberly flying onto the stage, she knew it could.

"Anna, I know you can do it," Daddy said, bending down to look carefully into Anna's eyes.

"All right," said Anna, finally.

"I think they're ready to begin. You stay with Kimberly and help her with her entrance. I'll join Mom in the audience."

Anna watched the stage lights go on, and listened as the buzz of the audience quieted. She heard Miss Crystal announce, "Ladies and gentlemen. A very dramatic incident occurred today. Anna Skoggen was to have been The Spinning Witch in tonight's performance. But this morning she broke her arm and is unable to perform her part. Anna's sister, Kimberly, will fill in for her." Miss Crystal paused dramatically. "And now . . . the third-grade class of Gibraltar School presents *Golden Wishes.*"

Anna walked over to Kimberly. Kimberly was standing next to the ladder. The stage makeup looked bloody red against Kimberly's pale white cheeks.

Kimberly and Anna stood alone in silence as Stephanie Bolter walked on stage and started her lines.

"Kimberly, climb up the ladder," began Anna, but then she cleared her throat. She tried again. "Kimberly, climb the ladder." But Kimberly remained on the ground. "Kimberly," she said. "Go on up." Still, Kimberly remained below.

"Kimberly!" Anna almost shouted.

Slowly, slowly Kimberly climbed the ladder. She stood near the top looking beyond the lights. She was gripping the top rung tightly with both hands. Anna looked up into Kimberly's face. Tears were streaking through the rouge on her cheeks. Kimberly was crying!

"What's wrong?" asked Anna.

Kimberly didn't answer. Anna climbed the ladder and asked again, "Kimberly, tell me what's wrong."

"I'm afraid."

"Of what?" asked Anna.

"Everything! I'm afraid to be up here and I'm afraid to fly in. I'm afraid to be anywhere that's high like trees or Ferris wheels or airplanes or ladders. I'm afraid of flying."

Anna couldn't believe Kimberly could be afraid of anything. She always seemed to be so sure of herself. But it was almost time for Kimberly to go on. Anna had to think of something—fast.

"Kimberly, just walk in. Forget about flying."

"I can't do that! If I walk in, everyone will ask me why. Then I'll have to say I was afraid and Mom and Daddy will be disappointed in me! Then they'll say, 'Oh, Kimberly! You'll have to learn to be more like Anna. Anna will try anything. Anna's a true adventurer.'"

Try anything! Adventurer! Anna held her breath, wanting to hear what Kimberly said over and over in her mind.

"Anna has such wonderful ideas! She's so

creative! Anna this, Anna that. I can't stand it anymore!"

"But Kimberly," said Anna, "you never get into trouble. I'm always doing stupid things. You're beautiful and talented. I thought you were the special one! I thought Mom and Daddy wanted *me* to be like *you*!"

Kimberly and Anna looked at each other with wide eyes, like they hadn't ever really seen each other before.

One thing was clear to Anna: Kimberly was supposed to fly onstage in just a few minutes and it was up to Anna to help her. Part of Anna wanted Kimberly to blow it, to walk instead of fly. But another part of Anna—a new part—found the right thing to say.

"Kimberly," she said, "the rope is strong and you won't fall. I've tried it a million times. Just close your eyes and don't look down. Think of butterflies floating in." Kimberly looked at Anna doubtfully. "Think of butterflies, Kimberly, *mauve* butterflies. I know you can do it!"

Anna nodded to Collin and the curtains parted.

"Fly, butterfly!" she whispered to Kimberly, and Kimberly did.

Kimberly flew in and landed beside the sleeping Lilah. The audience gasped at her spectacular entrance and then began to applaud. Kimberly looked over at Anna, a smile slowly spreading over her face.

Anna knew the applause was for her, too. Kimberly had flown in, but Anna had helped her.

When the play was over, the whole cast appeared onstage for curtain calls. When Miss Crystal announced, "Kimberly Skoggen as The Spinning Witch," Kimberly walked over to Anna and took her hand. Then Kimberly and Anna walked onstage together.

The stage lights were bright, and Anna had to squint to see Mom and Daddy in the audience. There they were! They were smiling and applauding.

Miss Crystal walked to the front of the stage. She cleared her throat. "If you look in your program you'll see Anna Skoggen's name as The Spinning Witch. But Anna was not only an actress. She made the play truly special.

She added some special effects like the smoke and the lights and the flying. She's quite a creative stage technician. Anna, please take a bow."

Kimberly let go of Anna's hand so she could step to the front. Mom and Daddy smiled widely with pride. Then the applause began, this time for her. Anna listened as it swelled— loud, rumbling applause like waves upon the sand.